Word Wise with Wordsworth

as easy as pie—simple or straightforward (**idiom, page 24**)

adapt—to change something to make it more suitable (**verb, page 11**)

ambitious—having a strong desire to achieve a certain goal (**adjective, page 22**)

bonus—an extra unexpected gift or advantage (**noun, page 29**)

certainly—without a doubt (**adverb, page 16**)

coax—to gently try to get someone to do something (**verb, page 12**)

confidence—a feeling of certainty or trust in one's abilities (**noun, page 18**)

contain—to hold something (**verb, page 18,** *contains*)

diligent—showing persistence and hard work (**adjective, page 7**)

distinctive—different or unusual (**adjective, page 8**)

edible—safe to eat (**adjective, page 20**)

finicky—extremely fussy or picky (**adjective, page 13**)

fluke—something surprising that happens by accident (**noun, page 9**)

grateful—feeling thankful (**adjective, page 22**)

improvise—to do something without any preparation (**verb, page 15,** *improvised*)

quantity—the total amount or number (**noun, page 25**)

remarkable—worth remembering, extraordinary (**adjective, page 26**)

scamper—to run quickly or playfully (**verb, page 11,** *scampered*)

scrumptious—very pleasing, especially to the taste (**adjective, page 20**)

vacant—empty, not filled (**adjective, page 14**)

zeal—energetic enthusiasm or eagerness (**noun, page 26**)

As Easy as Pie

by Quinn Alexander
Illustrated by Kelly Kennedy

SCHOLASTIC INC.

New York Toronto London Auckland Sydney
Mexico City New Delhi Hong Kong Buenos Aires

Mrs. Harris said, "Good-bye, class," as they left at the end of another day at Webster Elementary School. "Remember you have a spelling test tomorrow, so study hard."

Wordsworth, the class pet, stopped shredding the newspapers in the bottom of his birdcage to echo Mrs. Harris. "Study hard! Study hard!" he called.

Two of the students, Abby and Marco, didn't leave with the rest of the class. They wanted to continue working on their history project about Cloverhill, the town where they lived. They got out their books and papers and took them to the table by Wordsworth's cage.

"I'm really impressed by how **diligent** you two are," Mrs. Harris said. "You've put in a lot of time on this project, and I think you deserve a treat!" She held up a bag of Aunt Franny's Favorite Cookies from the town bakery.

"Thanks, Mrs. Harris," said Marco.

"We love Aunt Franny's," said Abby.

The kids each took a big cookie and chewed happily. Mrs. Harris took one, too. "Mmm, I wonder what's in these," she said. "They have such a **distinctive** taste."

"I bet they would go well with your coffee," said Abby.

"Yeah. We'll be OK on our own, if you want to get some from the teachers' room," Marco added quickly.

"Good idea," said Mrs. Harris. "I'll be right back."

This was what Abby and Marco—and Wordsworth—had been waiting for. The moment Mrs. Harris left, the bird spread his wings and burst out, "Open the door! Open the door!"

"Yes!" shouted Marco, pumping his fist in the air. He scrambled to open the cage. Then—just as they had done every afternoon since this history project began—the three of them raced out of the room.

Mr. Keys, the school custodian, was at the end of the hall, standing on a ladder to change a light bulb. He had his back to them, and he was singing loudly, so he didn't notice them at all.

It was no **fluke** that Wordsworth headed straight for the supply shelves in the back of Mr. Keys's room. That's where the magic passageway to the past was located. Abby and Marco followed; and as before, the shelves melted away into a dark tunnel. The students braced themselves. *Pop! Flash!*

Abby and Marco blinked. It took a minute for their eyes to **adapt** to the bright light. As usual, they were wearing clothes that were popular a hundred years ago.

"I guess I won't be playing baseball on this visit," Abby said. "But at least my dress is a different color than before."

She took a good look around. Wordsworth was perched on a branch of the huge tree next to them. There were only a few houses lining the street, and the closest one looked familiar.

"Marco, that's where my grandmother used to live!" Abby said, pointing. "I know exactly where we are. We're in our own neighborhood—*before* our houses were built!"

"That's an excellent observation, Abby," said Wordsworth. He was part of the conversation now, as he always was when they traveled back in time.

Yip, yip, yip! All of a sudden a small fluffy dog ran by, her ears flapping and her tail wagging.

"Tillie! Tillie, come back," a woman called.

Abby and Marco looked up and down the street, but they couldn't see who was calling. In the meantime, the dog **scampered** around the corner and out of sight.

"Did you hear that?" said Marco. "I bet that little dog is Tillie. Let's catch her!" He and Abby took off, while Wordsworth watched from the tree.

Abby tried to grab Tillie, but the dog stayed out of reach. Marco got down on his knees and tried to **coax** her to come by calling her name. But that didn't work either.

Suddenly a sharp whistle pierced the air. It was Wordsworth!

Tillie's ears perked up at the sound. She zigged when Abby zagged and headed back around the corner. The kids ran, panting, behind her. From the other direction, a short, rather plump woman arrived, also quite out of breath.

Yip, yip, yip! Tillie was barking up the tree where Wordsworth had been perched a moment before. But there was no sign of the cockatoo.

"Tillie! Where are your manners?" said the woman. She tugged on Tillie's collar, and the dog licked her hand and sat at her feet. "For that matter, where are *my* manners?" she continued. "I'm Mrs. Frances Murray, and this is Tillie, my young and—it turns out—rather **finicky** puppy. I offered her a freshly baked cookie that she clearly didn't like. She ran right out the front door and down the street." Mrs. Murray smiled at the kids. "Thank you for going after her. Won't you come back to my house for some homemade cookies and lemonade?"

Marco and Abby looked at each other. Wordsworth had disappeared. That was the signal that their adventure had begun, and they were supposed to go with Mrs. Murray.

"Thanks," said Marco. "That would be nice."

After they introduced themselves, the kids followed Mrs. Murray to her house. "She reminds me of someone, but I don't know who," Abby whispered to Marco.

"I was thinking the same thing," Marco whispered back.

Mrs. Murray's house was full of moving crates and cartons. She was quick to apologize for the mess, as she led the way to the kitchen. "My dear husband, Mr. Murray, passed away recently, and the house felt so **vacant**, I got little Tillie to keep me company," she said. "Unfortunately, I can't afford to live here anymore, so we have to move." She sighed and set a plate of cookies and a pitcher of lemonade on the table. "My niece over in Franklin wants me to come live with her and her family, but I would really rather stay in Cloverhill."

As Mrs. Murray turned to get some glasses from the cabinet, Marco took a cookie and bit into it. *Yeeouch!* It was really hard. Now he understood why Tillie had bolted. But he didn't want to hurt Mrs. Murray's feelings, so he **improvised**. He slipped the cookie into his shirt pocket, and when she came back with the glasses, he pretended to chew.

Abby had seen him hide the cookie. She looked at him, eyes wide, as she poured herself a glass of lemonade. She took a big swallow and started to cough. There was no sugar in the lemonade, which Mrs. Murray herself realized the second she took a sip.

"Oh, dear," said Mrs. Murray. "Here, have a bite of cookie to take away the sour taste." She tried to break a cookie in half, but it was too hard. "I'm so sorry. I usually make good lemonade—and soft, chewy cookies—as my niece's children would **certainly** tell you," she said. "But my recipes are all packed away, and I guess I have got too much on my mind to make even my favorite cookies without them."

"Favorite cookies," thought Abby. "There is something about Mrs. Murray and favorite cookies that seems *soooo* familiar."

"Frances—Franny—that's it!" Abby blurted out. "You're Aunt Franny of Aunt Franny's Favorite Cookies!"

Marco gave Abby a sharp poke. "She isn't Aunt Franny—yet," he hissed.

Luckily, Mrs. Murray wasn't listening. She was pouring the lemonade down the sink and dumping the cookies into the trash. She was clearly lost in thought.

Abby and Marco looked at each other.

"I know why we're here," whispered Marco.

"Me, too," Abby whispered back.

It was up to them to help Mrs. Murray *become* Aunt Franny of Aunt Franny's Favorite Cookies.

"Do you think we can find your recipes and make another batch of cookies?" Abby asked Mrs. Murray. "I'm sure they would be delicious."

Mrs. Murray nodded. "I know what each and every moving carton **contains**, dear. I'm very organized, though it may not appear that way now." She held up a notepad. "You see? I have a list. Each carton is numbered and its contents are recorded."

Just looking at the list seemed to give Mrs. Murray a small boost of **confidence**. "You are so sweet," she said to Abby. "And you both surely deserve a good batch of cookies and some drinkable lemonade. Let's find those recipes!"

Mrs. Murray led the way into the living room, with Tillie right at her heels. She checked her list. "I need box number 11. Do you see it?"

Abby and Marco poked around. "Here it is," said Marco. He moved the box to an open space on the floor. Tillie began scratching at its side.

Mrs. Murray laughed. "OK. OK. We'll open it, Tillie."

In no time at all, the recipes had been located and taken back to the kitchen. As Mrs. Murray read down the list of ingredients, she moved with ease around her kitchen. She pulled out bowls and measuring spoons and went from the icebox to the cupboard for supplies. Tillie ran in circles around her, yipping at her ankles.

"Goodness, Tillie. This is not helping," said Mrs. Murray. She turned to Marco and Abby and suggested, "Maybe you could take her to the backyard to play."

The kids had fun tossing sticks for Tillie, who had more energy than the two of them combined. Soon the smell of freshly baked cookies came through the open window, and they all went back into the kitchen.

Mrs. Murray held out a plate of cookies. "Now," she said, "tell me if *these* are **edible**." Then she smiled, because she already knew the answer.

The cookies were **scrumptious**! They tasted exactly like the ones Mrs. Harris had given Abby and Marco back at school. Mrs. Murray's recipe had stood the test of time.

Tillie stood on her hind legs, trying to reach the cookie in Marco's hand. Her nose sniffed in and out as fast as it could go.

"See, *now* Tillie wants a cookie!" said Marco.

"Then you may give her one," said Mrs. Murray. She put a fresh pitcher of lemonade on the table and poured a glass for everyone.

Abby took a cautious sip. The lemonade was cold and refreshing and tart and sweet at the same time. "It's perfect," she said.

Marco nodded. "You sure were right, Mrs. Murray," he said. "You *do* make terrific cookies and lemonade!"

"Thank you, dear," said Mrs. Murray. "Thank you both. I'm so **grateful** to you for reminding me that there are things I'm good at. And even if making cookies and lemonade is a small thing in life, it reminds me of happier times. That's why I tried to make them earlier today."

"I don't think making good cookies is a small thing," said Abby.

"Me, either," said Marco. "I think it could be a really big deal."

"What do you mean by that, dear?" Mrs. Murray asked.

"I just *know* that you could sell these cookies to everyone in town," said Abby.

Mrs. Murray looked astonished. "Sell my cookies?" she asked. "Don't you think that's quite **ambitious**?"

"No way!" said Marco. "Let's take them to the store where you buy your groceries. If you give the owner a taste, I bet he'll want to sell them."

Mrs. Murray didn't seem totally convinced. But Marco and Abby could see she was thinking hard. "Why not?" she finally said. "Besides, it's time for Tillie's walk. Let's get her leash and give it a try."

With Marco holding Tillie's leash and Abby and Mrs. Murray carefully carrying plates of cookies, the group walked to Jenkins' General Store on Washington Avenue.

Abby made the sales pitch. "Mr. Jenkins, we would like you to try an amazing cookie," she said. "Kids love them—and dogs do, too. We think you should sell them in your store."

"I'm always happy to try something new," said Mr. Jenkins. He took a cookie and tasted it.

Marco, Abby, and Mrs. Murray held their breath. Tillie panted and wagged her tail.

"These are the best cookies I've ever had!" Mr. Jenkins declared. "It'll be **as easy as pie** to sell them."

Abby and Marco walked back to the house with Mrs. Murray and Tillie. Mr. Jenkins had ordered a huge **quantity** of cookies, and Mrs. Murray could hardly believe her good fortune. "Did you hear Mr. Jenkins say that they would be 'as easy as pie to sell'? Well, just wait until he tastes my *pies*! I have dozens of recipes for all kinds of desserts—cookies, pies, cakes, pastries . . . This means I can stay in Cloverhill. Maybe I'll even have my own bakery some day!"

She gave Abby and Marco a hug before she and Tillie went back into the house. She was going to start baking right away. But she invited the kids to come back soon. She said she would keep them well fed with sweet things.

Abby and Marco walked down the block to the place where they had last seen Wordsworth—and there he was, perched in the big tree. Mrs. Murray's newfound **zeal** had made the kids very happy, but they also felt bad that she was expecting them to come back.

"We probably won't ever see her again," said Abby. "But we couldn't tell her that."

"Cheer up," said Wordsworth. "She'll always remember the two **remarkable** kids who helped her find her way forward. And after all, she *does* keep you well fed *now*, doesn't she?"

It was time to go home. "Open the door," said Wordsworth.

The closest house was the one that had belonged to Abby's grandmother. It had several doors, but the kids didn't have a clue which one to open.

Then Abby had an idea. "There used to be a shed behind the house," she said. "Let's give that a try."

Wordsworth hopped onto Marco's shoulder, and the three walked around the house. Sure enough, there was the shed. Abby opened the door, and with a pop and a flash of bright light, they were back in Mr. Keys's room.

The custodian was still at the end of hall, still on the ladder with his back to them. As before, even though they had spent hours in Cloverhill of the past, they had only been gone from the school for an instant.

Wordsworth flew ahead of the kids, back to the classroom and into his cage. Marco closed the door. Then he and Abby rushed to look at the old map of Cloverhill.

A bakery had been added to it—Aunt Franny's Bakery!

They looked at the bag of cookies Mrs. Harris had brought. On it was a picture of Aunt Franny. She was older than the Mrs. Murray they had met, but they recognized her right away. Next to her in the picture was an older, plumper version of Tillie, surrounded by four adorable puppies.

Suddenly Marco remembered the cookie he had put in his pocket. It was still there. He examined it carefully. It was made of tightly packed nuts, seeds, and raisins—all things that Wordsworth liked. He gave the cookie to the cockatoo. "Here's a **bonus** for you, Wordsworth," Marco said.

Wordsworth took a bite just as Mrs. Harris came back to the classroom. "Good!" he squawked.

"That's nice. We all have an afternoon treat," said Mrs. Harris, taking a sip of her coffee.

Wordsworth took another bite. He swallowed and bobbed his head. "Good work!" he said. Then he went back to his cookie.

Get Your Word's Worth

After you finish reading this book together, use the prompts below to spark thoughtful conversation and lively interaction with your child.

- ♣ Someone who is **distinctive** stands out above others. Explain why you think you are distinctive.

- ♣ Show me how you would act or what you would say to show that you are **grateful** for a gift I gave you.

- ♣ By now, Marco and Abby know it's not a **fluke** that they travel to the past. Tell me about a time when you have experienced a fluke.

- ♣ Let's **improvise** and make up a 1-minute play or skit about Marco and Abby.